Dyeing

A skillfully prepared vat of indigo dye can last for years and is a precious possession of the textile maker. To make a vat of indigo dye, the dye-maker mixes dried indigo paste, lye, and water. The mixture is warmed and carefully tended— sometimes for a month or more—until it is ready for use. The fabric to be dyed is dipped into water and then into the dye vat and then is hung to dry. This process may be repeated many times. Depending upon the number of dippings, indigo-dyed fabric may be light blue to deep navy blue.

Indigo

For more than 4000 years, the weavers and dyers of the world have made rich blue indigo dye from plants they found growing wild or which they grew in small plots near their homes. In Japan, the most common source of natural indigo dye has been a plant called dyer's knotweed. Following an ancient procedure, the dye-maker strips the leaves from the plants, wets the leaves, covers them, and allows them to ferment. Then the fermented leaves are pounded to a paste in a mortar and formed into lumps, called indigo balls. These indigo balls are then dried and stored until needed. Around the world, natural and synthetic indigo remains one of the most popular dyes, coloring everything from blue jeans to silk scarves.

Stenciling

Stenciling is a traditional Japanese technique for applying designs to cloth. Before the fabric is dyed, designs are stenciled on with wax or rice paste. When the fabric is dipped in dye, the wax or paste keeps the fabric from absorbing the dye in the stenciled areas. After the fabric is dyed, the wax or paste is washed out. The circular designs illustrated here are typical Japanese stencil patterns.

Kimono

The manufacture of textiles is a major industry in Japan, but a few individual craftspeople still make durable handmade and hand-decorated fabrics. These fabrics are especially popular for the kimono—the traditional Japanese garment for men and women. The kimono is a long loose robe, tied at the waist with a sash called an obi. Even though most Japanese people have adopted Western-style clothing, traditional clothing is often worn on special occasions.

HANA'S YEAR

Written by **Carol Talley**

Illustrated by **Itoko Maeno**

MarshMedia, Kansas City, Missouri

To Mozu, a brave-spirited macaque monkey

First Printing 1992
Second Printing 1998
Third Printing 2000

Published by MARSH media
A Division of Marsh Film Enterprises, Inc.
P. O. Box 8082
Shawnee Mission, KS 66208

Library of Congress Cataloging-in-Publication Data

Talley, Carol.
Hana's year / written by Carol Talley; illustrated by Itoko Maeno.
p. cm.
Summary: A young macaque monkey living in the mountains of Japan gets into trouble when she follows the lead of a mischief-maker. Includes discussion questions on peer pressure and information on Japanese folk textiles.
ISBN 1-55942-034-0
1. Japanese macaque—Juvenile fiction. [1. Japanese macaque—Fiction. 2. Monkeys—Fiction. 3. Japan—Fiction. 4. Peer pressure—Fiction.] I. Maeno, Itoko, ill. II. Title.
PZ10.3.T1382Han 1992
[Fic]—dc20 92-19290

Book layout and typography by Cirrus Design

Printed in Hong Kong

Special thanks to David L. Knight, Theodore Otteson, Linda Talley, and Wilma Yeo.

Springtime came to Japan. A thousand birds soared through the bright air, and the mountainside smiled with cherry blossoms.

On this mountainside lived a monkey named Hana. Hana was one year old. More and more she left her mother's side to play with other little monkeys—Kiku and Matsu and Nashi and Beni. And Tampopo.

Tampopo was a mischief-maker, but she did not enjoy getting into trouble alone. Her favorite words were "Follow me!" And many little monkeys followed Tampopo into all kinds of trouble.

One day, Hana found herself right behind Kiku and Matsu, Nashi and Beni, climbing the greening branches of the tallest tree on the mountainside. Suddenly Hana was afraid. If she cried out now, her mother would not be able to hear her.

"Follow me!" came Tampopo's cry from above. Hana climbed on, higher than she had ever climbed before, then higher than that—all the way to the top. And then, what did it matter that she could not see her mother? She could see the whole world! Mountains and streams and a valley and, in the valley, something none of the little monkeys had ever seen before—a house and, beside the house, a woman hoeing in her garden.

Then the house seemed to turn upside down. But it was Hana who was upside down. She was falling, crashing through the branches of the tallest tree she had ever climbed.

When Hana opened her eyes, she didn't know where she was. Hana had never been in a house before. How could she understand four walls or the woman working in the corner or the clack, clack, clack of her loom? Or the boy looking down at her? "O-saru," he said. "Honorable monkey."

Then Kenji, for that was the boy's name, held a bowl of water to Hana's lips. "I see your monkey is feeling better," said Kenji's grandmother, for that's who she was.

For two days, Kenji nursed the young monkey. And Kenji, who seldom had anyone new to talk to, told Hana about his life, how he and his grandmother grew and harvested hemp, how his grandmother spun the hemp fibers into thread and worked at her loom all year to weave the thread into a few bolts of kimono cloth, how together they dipped the cloth into indigo dye and rinsed it in the stream to set the color, and how beautiful the blue cloth was and how prized.

When Hana was well again, Kenji carried her back to the foot of the tall tree. Tying a strip of indigo blue cloth around her neck in token of friendship and bowing politely, he sent her on her way.

Of course Hana's mother was happy to have her child safely home. "But Hana," she said, "following Tampopo into trouble was a mistake. Everyone makes mistakes, and even a monkey may sometimes fall from a tree. But don't make the same mistake a second time. Don't rely on Tampopo's judgment. Use your own."

It was summertime when Tampopo determined to go down to the valley herself. "Let's go see what's growing in the old woman's garden," she said.

"I want to see the garden!" cried Beni.

"We have plenty to eat right here," protested Hana, "nuts and cicadas and leaves and a hundred other things fit for monkeys." But Hana knew that Tampopo was not looking for food. She was looking for trouble.

"We can go without Hana," said Tampopo with a sly, sidelong look. "Can't we Kiku and Nashi? Can't we Matsu and Beni?" Hana wavered.

"Whoever wants an adventure, follow me!" called Tampopo, already leaping and bounding through the trees. And Hana, who did not want to be left behind, forgot her mother's words and followed.

Where Kenji's grandmother had hoed the dirt in springtime, there were now flowers and herbs and ripe vegetables. It was Tampopo who pulled the first fat tomato from its vine and tossed it at Kiku. Kiku retaliated with a shiny purple eggplant. It missed Tampopo and struck Nashi on the nose. A cabbage bowled Matsu off his feet, and a cucumber knocked Beni into the beans.

And then above the clamor of screaming monkeys came a new uproar. Here came Kenji, calling out and waving his arms wildly. Here came Kenji's grandmother beating on a pot with a big wooden spoon. Down came the spoon on every monkey head she could reach. Monkeys flew in every direction. Hana bolted around the corner of the house. And there she stopped.

What she saw made Hana forget all about the shattered garden, the arm-waving boy, the pot-pounding grandmother. It was an enchanting sight—yards and yards of indigo blue rippling in the breeze. Hana had never seen anything so pretty.

Then Hana saw Tampopo. Tampopo, too, was looking at the blue kimono cloth. But just as she reached out her greedy paw to touch it, an angry cry sent her scrambling through the bushes. Hana looked up to see the fierce Kenji. This time he did not bow to Hana. He did not call her honorable monkey.

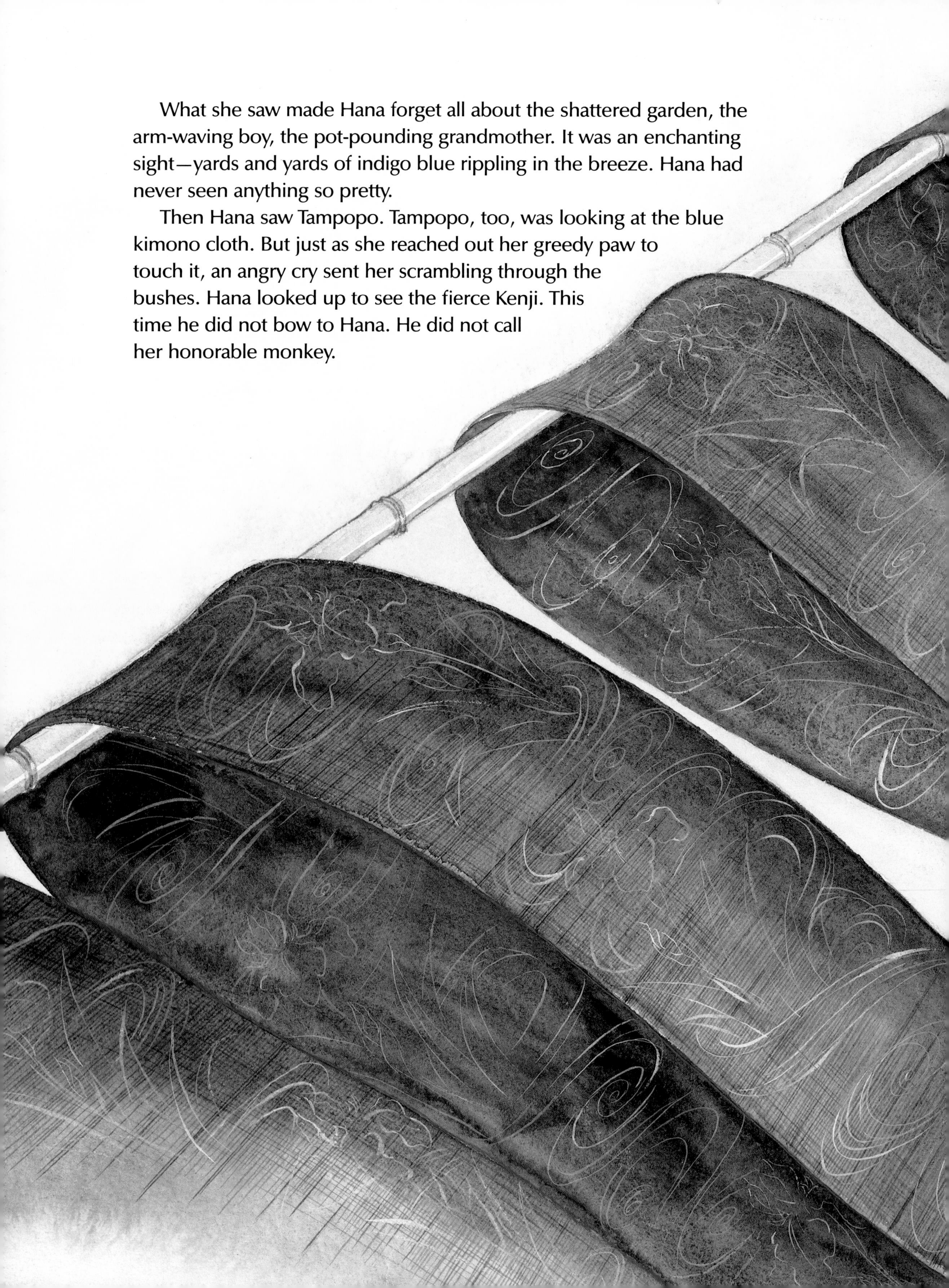

Hana fled in shame—past Kenji, past his grandmother weeping in her ruined garden, and into the trees.

Hana did not tell her mother how she had followed Tampopo into trouble a second time.

Often now, Hana was alone.
She stayed behind when Tampopo lured
Kiku and Matsu, Nashi and Beni deep into a
mountain cave. She watched from the bank as they
floated off down a mountain stream on a fallen tree trunk.

Who could have known that the little monkeys would wander lost for more than a day before finding their way out of the cave? Or that they would almost drown when the tree trunk carried them over a raging cataract?

Hana had learned her lesson. She would not follow Tampopo into trouble again.

Summer turned to autumn. The trees turned to crimson and gold. Chestnuts and ripe persimmons fell from their branches. The woodpecker's tat tat tat echoed through the mist.

One day, bored with tumbling in the red and gold leaves, Tampopo began to think about the house in the valley and the blue kimono cloth rippling in the breeze. "I'll bet even Hana will follow me this time," she said, turning to where only a moment before Hana had been sitting looking troubled. But Hana had disappeared.

Sometimes it is not easy for a little monkey to do a good deed. How difficult it was for Hana to find Kenji and his grandmother in the far field where they were harvesting the hemp. How they shoo-ed Hana away. How they slapped her paw as she tugged at their jackets. And even when Kenji and his grandmother shrugged and laid down their sickles—how ploddingly they followed the persistent little monkey across the hemp field toward home. But Kenji broke into a run when he saw two monkeys disappear around the corner of his house.

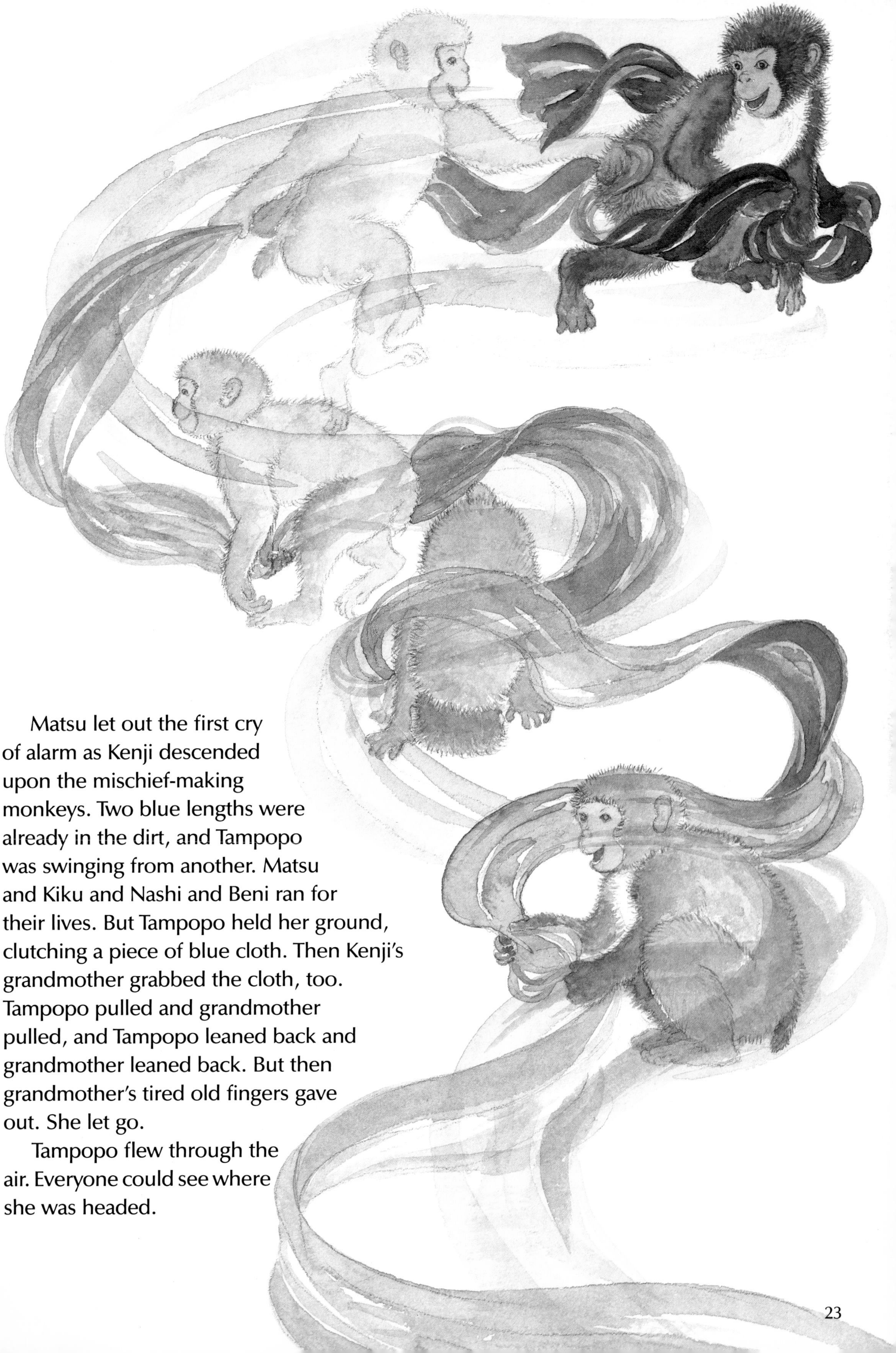

Matsu let out the first cry of alarm as Kenji descended upon the mischief-making monkeys. Two blue lengths were already in the dirt, and Tampopo was swinging from another. Matsu and Kiku and Nashi and Beni ran for their lives. But Tampopo held her ground, clutching a piece of blue cloth. Then Kenji's grandmother grabbed the cloth, too. Tampopo pulled and grandmother pulled, and Tampopo leaned back and grandmother leaned back. But then grandmother's tired old fingers gave out. She let go.

Tampopo flew through the air. Everyone could see where she was headed.

And then Tampopo splashed down into the open vat of indigo dye.

How grateful Kenji and his grandmother were that Hana had saved the kimono cloth. Hana would always remember that day—how grandmother patted the top of her head and how Kenji bowed to her once again. "O-saru-sama," he said. "*Very* honorable monkey."

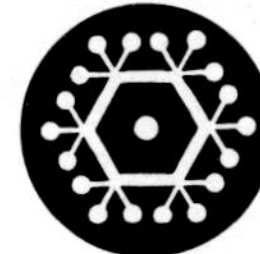

Winter came to the mountainside. The wind whistled through the pine boughs and shook the bare branches of the oak and maple. The snow grew deep. On many days, the monkeys— young and old—huddled together for warmth.

But this was one of those magical days when the wind held its breath and icicles sparkled in wintery sunshine. Hana was almost two years old now. She and the other young monkeys had played all morning in the bright, white snow, and now they were resting near their mothers. Hana picked up a lump of snow to eat. But then she stopped and did an unusual thing.

She rolled the lump gently over the snow. As she did, it grew larger. She pushed it a little further, and it grew larger still. Kiku and Matsu and Nashi and Beni and all the monkeys watched Hana and watched her snowball grow and grow. "What an amazing discovery!" said one of the mothers. Hana's mother was inclined to agree.

"What a remarkable monkey!" said another. Hana's mother believed it was true. Soon other young monkeys were rolling snowballs.

One monkey, however, was slow to join in. She didn't like to be a follower. She was—in her own way—a remarkable monkey, too. "Come on!" called Hana. "Join the fun!"

And finally even Tampopo couldn't resist following Hana.

Dear Parents and Educators:

Just say "No."
Choose to refuse.

With messages like these we encourage our children to resist peer pressure and to take responsibility for their own actions. Nevertheless, even our best-intentioned children often listen to others to determine what they ought to do, how they ought to behave, what values they should adhere to. Why?

Much could be said about the power of the media, the disorder in our schools and neighborhoods, the disintegration of our families—and the roles these play in making followers of our children. But we might also look at two other messages our young people receive from an early age:

The majority rules.
Respect authority.

In our democratic society, children learn early the weight of the majority opinion. They vote at school for class officers and at home to determine the destination of the family vacation. Is it surprising then that children too often look to the group to make their decisions for them? To help children learn to make responsible personal choices, we must help them distinguish between the legitimate power of the majority in politics and its illegitimate power over their *thinking*.

Young people also learn early that they are to respect the authority of their parents and teachers. The danger is that obedience will become a habit of mind, making the child easy prey for the Tampopos of the world, who seem to speak with the voice of authority. There is an old saying that good judgment comes from experience, and experience comes from bad judgment. Sound decision-making takes practice. We need to give children the freedom to make a few mistakes, to occasionally—like Hana—fall from a tree.

Hana's Year shows children that the group does not always make the right choice, that not every strong and confident voice is to be obeyed, and that even a good-hearted little monkey may make a few mistakes before learning these lessons.

To help youngsters better understand the message of *Hana's Year,* discuss the following questions with them:

- Do you know a mischief-maker like Tampopo?
- Why do you suppose mischief-makers like company when they get into trouble?
- Why do you think Hana followed Tampopo and the other monkeys into trouble a second time?
- Why was Hana often alone after she decided not to follow Tampopo into trouble again?
- Why did Tampopo follow Hana's example at the end of the story?
- Can you remember a time when you were a follower? A leader? What happened?

Here are some ways you can help children learn to resist peer pressure and think for themselves:

- Distinguish between decisions which are rightly determined by the majority and those that are personal and individual.
- Discuss who has authority over the child and the limits to that authority.
- Allow young people opportunities to make decisions. Decision-making takes practice.
- Prepare children for dangerous situations—such as the offer of drugs—by role-playing.
- Help turn mistakes in judgment into learning experiences.

Available from MarshMedia

These storybooks, each hardcover with dust jacket and full-color illustrations throughout, are available at bookstores, or you may order by calling MarshMedia toll free at 1-800-821-3303.

Amazing Mallika, written by Jami Parkison, illustrated by Itoko Maeno. 32 pages. ISBN 1-55942-087-1.

Bailey's Birthday, written by Elizabeth Happy, illustrated by Andra Chase. 32 pages. ISBN 1-55942-059-6.

Bastet, written by Linda Talley, illustrated by Itoko Maeno. 32 pages. ISBN 1-55942-161-4.

Bea's Own Good, written by Linda Talley, illustrated by Andra Chase. 32 pages. ISBN 1-55942-092-8.

Clarissa, written by Carol Talley, illustrated by Itoko Maeno. 32 pages. ISBN 1-55942-014-6.

Emily Breaks Free, written by Linda Talley, illustrated by Andra Chase. 32 pages. ISBN 1-55942-155-X.

Feathers at Las Flores, written by Linda Talley, illustrated by Andra Chase. 32 pages. ISBN 1-55942-162-2.

Following Isabella, written by Linda Talley, illustrated by Andra Chase. 32 pages. ISBN 1-55942-163-0.

Gumbo Goes Downtown, written by Carol Talley, illustrated by Itoko Maeno. 32 pages. ISBN 1-55942-042-1.

Hana's Year, written by Carol Talley, illustrated by Itoko Maeno. 32 pages. ISBN 1-55942-034-0.

Inger's Promise, written by Jami Parkison, illustrated by Andra Chase. 32 pages. ISBN 1-55942-080-4.

Jackson's Plan, written by Linda Talley, illustrated by Andra Chase. 32 pages. ISBN 1-55942-104-5.

Jomo and Mata, written by Alyssa Chase, illustrated by Andra Chase. 32 pages. ISBN 1-55942-051-0.

Kiki and the Cuckoo, written by Elizabeth Happy, illustrated by Andra Chase. 32 pages. ISBN 1-55942-038-3.

Kylie's Concert, written by Patty Sheehan, illustrated by Itoko Maeno. 32 pages. ISBN 1-55942-046-4.

Kylie's Song, written by Patty Sheehan, illustrated by Itoko Maeno. 32 pages. (Advocacy Press) ISBN 0-911655-19-0.

Minou, written by Mindy Bingham, illustrated by Itoko Maeno. 64 pages. (Advocacy Press) ISBN 0-911655-36-0.

Molly's Magic, written by Penelope Colville Paine, illustrated by Itoko Maeno. 32 pages. ISBN 1-55942-068-5.

My Way Sally, written by Mindy Bingham and Penelope Paine, illustrated by Itoko Maeno. 48 pages. (Advocacy Press) ISBN 0-911655-27-1.

Papa Piccolo, written by Carol Talley, illustrated by Itoko Maeno. 32 pages. ISBN 1-55942-028-6.

Pequeña the Burro, written by Jami Parkison, illustrated by Itoko Maeno. 32 pages. ISBN 1-55942-055-3.

Plato's Journey, written by Linda Talley, illustrated by Itoko Maeno. 32 pages. ISBN 1-55942-100-2.

Tessa on Her Own, written by Alyssa Chase, illustrated by Itoko Maeno. 32 pages. ISBN 1-55942-064-2.

Thank You, Meiling, written by Linda Talley, illustrated by Itoko Maeno. 32 pages. ISBN 1-55942-118-5.

Time for Horatio, written by Penelope Paine, illustrated by Itoko Maeno. 48 pages. (Advocacy Press) ISBN 0-911655-33-6.

Toad in Town, written by Linda Talley, illustrated by Itoko Maeno. 32 pages. ISBN 1-55942-165-7.

Tonia the Tree, written by Sandy Stryker, illustrated by Itoko Maeno. 32 pages. (Advocacy Press) ISBN 0-911655-16-6.

Companion videos and activity guides, as well as multimedia kits for classroom use, are also available. MarshMedia has been publishing high-quality, award-winning learning materials for children since 1969. To order or to receive a free catalog, call 1-800-821-3303, or visit us at www.marshmedia.com.

Japanese Folk Textiles

For centuries, country craftspeople of Japan have made durable, often beautiful, textiles for the clothes of farmers, fishermen, and their families. The techniques and materials used by these rural weavers and dyers have now given way to those required for the mass production of textiles. But a few folk artists still practice the ancient ways, producing small quantities of highly-prized traditional cloth.

Weaving

After the thread is made, it is woven into fabric on a loom. First, one set of threads, called the warp, is stretched taut on the loom. Then a second set of threads, called the weft, is interwoven, over and under the warp threads. A treadle loom like the one used by Kenji's grandmother makes this interweaving quick and easy. When one foot pedal is pressed down, all the even numbered warp threads are raised so that the weft thread may be passed under them. When the other foot pedal is pressed, the odd warp threads are raised and the weft thread is passed back. Thread by thread the fabric is created.

Hemp

Cloth can be made from animal fibers, such as the hair of sheep, goats, camels, and rabbits, or the filaments manufactured by silkworms; or from plant materials, such as cotton, flax, and jute. For more than 2000 years, the people of Japan have used the fibers in the stems of the hemp plant to make durable fabric for clothing and household items. The stems must be soaked in water to loosen the inner fibers from the bark. The hemp is then beaten against a hard surface or crushed with a wooden club to soften the fibers for spinning into thread.

Spinning

A small amount of thread can be made from animal or plant fibers just by drawing out a few fibers from a clump and twisting them between the fingers. The twisting holds the overlapping fibers together. If the end of the thread is fastened to a stick and the thread is wound onto the stick as it is made, it will not come untwisted, and a lengthy thread can be made. All hand-spinning tools, including the spinning wheel used by Kenji's grandmother, are elaborations on the simple stick of the first thread-makers.